CW00867728

SIR GAWAIN AND THE GREEN KNIGHT

Retold by Margaret Berrill
Illustrated by Susan Hunter

Methuen Children's Books
in association with Belitha Press Ltd.

IT WAS CHRISTMASTIME IN KING ARTHUR'S COURT AT CAMELOT.
For a full fortnight the most famous knights in all the world,
and the loveliest ladies too,
delighted in singing and dancing, in feasting and jousting,
and in giving gifts and playing Christmas games.
On New Year's Day a great feast was held
with double portions for all.
But Arthur himself would not sit down to eat
until he had heard of some great adventure,
or until some stranger should come to his court
and offer a challenge to one of his knights.

Note: The long poem on which this story is
based was written in the late fourteenth
century by an unknown poet in the language,
now called 'Middle English', from which
our own modern English developed. The
character of Gawain was known in old Irish
tales, and then appeared in stories about
King Arthur's court as the perfect knight.
But later other heroes became more
important, and in the famous stories of King
Arthur's court written by Sir Thomas
Malory, Gawain is not even a very
admirable character.

MB

Copyright © in this format Belitha Press Ltd, 1988
Text copyright © Margaret Berrill 1988
Illustrations copyright © Susan Hunter 1988
Art Director: Treld Bicknell
First published in Great Britain in 1988
by Methuen Children's Books Ltd,
11 New Fetter Lane, London EC4P 4EE
Conceived, designed and produced by Belitha Press Ltd,
31 Newington Green, London N16 9PU
ISBN 0 416 96250 5 (hardback)

Printed in Hong Kong by South China Printing Co.

The first course had just been served,
and everyone, except the king, was beginning to eat,
when, to their amazement, the doors opened and
a huge horseman came riding down the hall.
He seemed half giant, half man,
and never before had they seen such a sight,
for everything about the handsome knight was green.
In one hand he held a branch of green holly
to bring good luck at Christmastime, and in the other a huge green axe.
All the diners were silent and the stranger did not speak
until he reached the high table
where Arthur was standing near Queen Guinevere.

Then, glaring around, he demanded to know
who was lord of that company.

Arthur did not hesitate but politely replied,
"You are welcome, Sir Knight.
I am the king of this land, and Arthur is my name.
Please do us the honour of joining our feast."
The Green Knight answered that he did not mean to stay.
He had come in peace, as his holly branch showed,
to play a game at Christmastime.
"Let one of these brave knights take my axe
and strike one blow at me,
then in a year from now I shall have the right
to strike a return blow at him."
The company sat as if turned to stone,
and no one came forward to take up the challenge.
The Green Knight glared, and then laughed in scorn,
so that Arthur felt ashamed of his knights
and took the axe himself.
Then his nephew, Sir Gawain, spoke from the high table.
Of all Arthur's knights he was the most famous
for his bravery, skill in battle, and courtly behaviour.
"My lord, this game is too foolish for you to play.
Please permit me to leave my seat by the Queen,
and let the game be mine."
Then all agreed that Gawain should accept the challenge,
and he took hold of the axe.
"My name is Gawain," he told the Green Knight,
"and in a year's time I will receive a blow from you
in return for the one I am about to give.
But first tell me your name, and where I can find you."
"Just strike the blow now," the Green Knight replied.
"Afterwards I will tell you my name
and where you can find me.
If I cannot speak, so much the better for you,
for then you will not have to come and seek me out."
Then he bent his neck,
and Gawain raised the huge axe high in the air.

Down came the axe and the sharp blade
cut off the Green Knight's head.
It rolled away across the floor
but the Green Knight did not stagger or fall.
He strode across to pick up his head
then mounted his horse, and turning towards the high table,
the head began to speak.
"I am the Knight of the Green Chapel, Sir Gawain.
Next New Year's Day you must come to my home
to receive a blow like the one you gave me.
Do not fail to find me, or you will be known forever as a coward."
With that he gave a roar,
turned his horse about and galloped out of the hall,
and where he went to nobody knew.
Although Arthur was amazed,
he did not show it, but said to Guinevere,
"Do not be afraid, dear lady. This was just a Christmas game,
but a marvellous one, I must admit, so now I can sit down to eat."
They hung up the axe for all to see,
and there was feasting and music until the day ended.

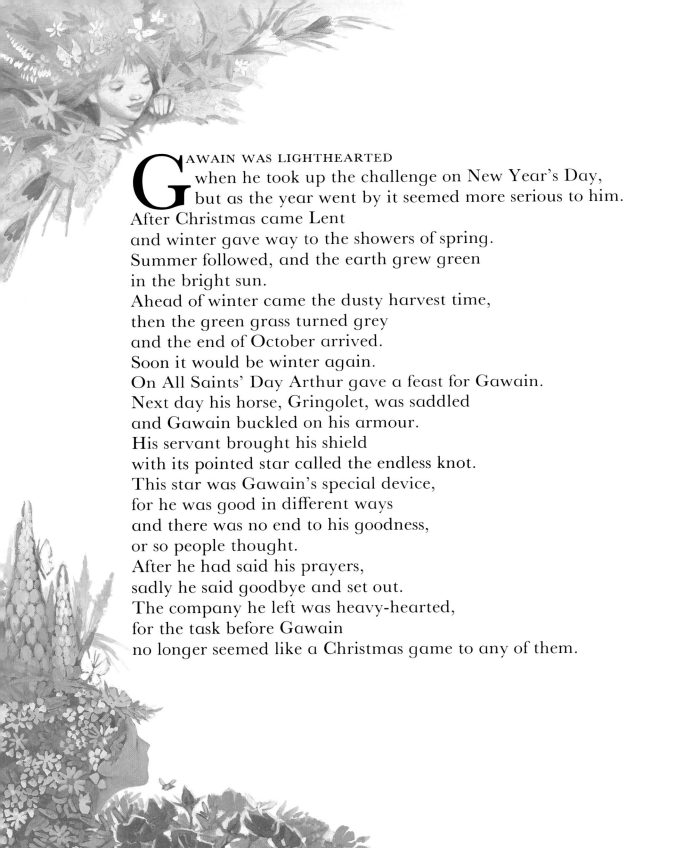

GAWAIN WAS LIGHTHEARTED
when he took up the challenge on New Year's Day,
but as the year went by it seemed more serious to him.
After Christmas came Lent
and winter gave way to the showers of spring.
Summer followed, and the earth grew green
in the bright sun.
Ahead of winter came the dusty harvest time,
then the green grass turned grey
and the end of October arrived.
Soon it would be winter again.
On All Saints' Day Arthur gave a feast for Gawain.
Next day his horse, Gringolet, was saddled
and Gawain buckled on his armour.
His servant brought his shield
with its pointed star called the endless knot.
This star was Gawain's special device,
for he was good in different ways
and there was no end to his goodness,
or so people thought.
After he had said his prayers,
sadly he said goodbye and set out.
The company he left was heavy-hearted,
for the task before Gawain
no longer seemed like a Christmas game to any of them.

FOR WEEKS GAWAIN RODE INTO STRANGE COUNTRYSIDE, always alone, with only Gringolet for company.
Wherever he went, he asked anyone he met,
"Can you tell me, sir, where I can find
the Green Knight who lives in the Green Chapel?"
But no one had ever heard of a Green Knight,
or knew where the Green Chapel might be.
On he went, into the wilderness of the Wirral,
over cliffs and across rivers,
and often he had to fight a dragon or a wolf,
or one of the trolls who lived among the crags.
There were bulls and bears, boars and ogres,
but worse than these was the winter weather.

Most nights he had to sleep among the rocks in his armour,
half dead with the cold and sleet.
At last came the morning of Christmas Eve,
and Gawain was worried that he would not be able
to go to church on Christmas Day.
So he prayed to Mary, the mother of Christ,
(whose picture was painted inside his shield
to give him courage in battle),
that she would lead him to some place
where he might find people living.

THAT SAME MORNING GAWAIN RODE ALONG A HILLSIDE
into a deep, wild forest,
and he had just prayed again to Mary
when suddenly he saw through the trees
a beautiful castle set high above a meadow surrounded by a moat.
When he rode up on Gringolet, the drawbridge was let down
and some of the company came out
and knelt on the cold ground to greet him.
The lord himself came to the great hall to make him welcome,
and Gawain thought that such a huge and handsome man
was fit to be the owner of so fine a castle
and the lord of so noble a company.

The servants led Gawain to a bedroom which was richly furnished,
and they gave him fine clothes to wear, and delicious food to eat.
With polite questions the company soon found out
that this was Sir Gawain, from the court of King Arthur,
who was so famous for his courtly behaviour
and courage in battle,
and they were delighted to have him
among them that Christmastime.

AS THE EVENING DREW ON, THEY ALL WENT TO CHAPEL.
The lord of the castle took Gawain with him
into a pew with his lovely young wife
and an ugly old lady who never left her side.
On Christmas Day, and for three days after,
there was dancing and singing, feasting and games,
and Gawain and the lady were most happy together.
But on the third day, Gawain knew that he must linger no longer,
and he said to the lord, "Tell me, Sir Knight,
if you know of a Green Knight who lives in a Green Chapel,
for I must find that place by New Year's Day,"
and he told the lord about the Green Knight's challenge.
"Stay here in comfort then until New Year's Day,"
replied the lord, roaring with laughter,
"for that Green Chapel is only two miles away!
Sleep on tomorrow as long as you like.
My wife will take care of you during the day.
I shall go hunting, and as it is Christmas, let us agree
that whatever I catch in the hunt shall be yours,
and in return you must give me
anything that may come your way at home!"
Gladly Sir Gawain agreed to this game.

NEXT MORNING, WHILE IT WAS STILL DARK,
the lord of the castle rode away to the hunt.
But Gawain lay dozing until the sun rose.
He heard a small sound and peeped through the bed's curtains
and saw the young lady steal into his room.
He lay down again and pretended to sleep.
She sat on his bed and, when he opened his eyes
and seemed to be surprised, she laughed very softly.
"You are my prisoner, Sir Gawain," she said,
and she stayed a long time speaking sweet words of love.
Gawain did not know what to do for the best,
but politely replied, and finally said,
"You honour me, madam, but praise me too highly.
Your husband is a far better man than I am."
"Perhaps after all you are not really Sir Gawain,"
said the lady with a laugh,
"for I feel sure that such a famous knight
would have asked for a kiss
from any lady who spent so long with him."
So, for fear of offending her, Gawain agreed,
and she kissed him sweetly and left the room.

ALL DAY LONG THE LORD, WITH A HUNDRED HORSEMEN,
their horns blaring and their hounds baying,
had chased up hill and down dale hunting a herd of deer.
At night they returned to the castle
and called the whole company into the hall,
to see how many deer they had killed and cut up
ready for the kitchen.
"All this must be yours, Sir Gawain, according to our agreement,"
cried the lord in a merry mood.
"Now tell me if you managed to catch anything at home
to give me in exchange!"
"All that I caught I will gladly give you," replied Gawain.
He put his arms around the lord's neck
and gave him a sweet kiss.
And they laughed about their bargain
and agreed that on the following day they would again exchange
whatever they might win in the hunt or at home.

ON THE SECOND DAY, BEFORE THE SUN ROSE,
the lord rode away with huntsmen and hounds,
while Gawain lay in his soft warm bed.
Again the lady came to him and offered her love,
and gave him two kisses before she would leave.
Her husband was on the track of a huge, fierce boar,
which knocked down some huntsmen who stood in its path
and wounded some hounds with its sharp tusks.
But the lord charged after it across country
on a fast horse all the day long,
and at last drove it into a hole in a bank by a stream.

Then the lord jumped into the water
and fought hard with the boar,
until he gave it a deadly wound with his sword.
So that night in the hall
the lord had a fine boar to give Gawain,
and, in return, Gawain gave him the two kisses
which the lady had given him that morning.
Then they sang and played games and were merry together,
and promised to make the same bargain again.
"For I have tested you twice
and found you true to your word," said the lord.

ON THE THIRD MORNING GAWAIN LAY ASLEEP
dreaming of the Green Chapel,
and the dreadful blow he must soon receive.
But the lady woke him with loving words,
then sadly said, "As you will not love me,
I think you left your love behind at Arthur's court."
And Gawain, afraid of offending her,
or doing wrong to her lord, sadly replied,
"Madam, I cannot give my love to any lady
for you know what lies before me tomorrow."
"At least take a gift to remember me by," she said.
"This green girdle may seem cheap to you,
but whoever wears it cannot be killed by any man on earth."
And she begged him to take it but to keep the gift secret.
That night the lord gave Gawain the skin of a fox,
and in return he received three kisses
as sweet as Gawain could make them,
just as the lady had given them to him that day.
But he kept the green girdle secret
and did not give that to the lord.
They feasted and danced till bedtime, then Gawain said goodbye,
and thanked the lord and his two ladies,
the young and the old, from the bottom of his heart
for all their kindness to him that Christmastime.

ON THE ICY COLD MORNING OF NEW YEAR'S DAY,
Gawain put on his armour
and wound the green girdle twice round his waist
in the hope that it might save his life.
His guide led him out into wild rough country,
then begged him not to go on to the Green Chapel.
But Gawain replied that whatever might happen
he must go to meet the Green Knight,
or know in his heart forever that he was a coward.
So he rode on down the track alone into a rocky valley
until he came to an old cave by a stream, all overgrown with grass.
"Can this strange place be the Green Chapel?"
wondered Gawain as he walked all around it.
Then, echoing from the cliffs, came a terrible sound
as though some huge weapon was being sharpened,
so he called out,
"Is the master of this place at home?
I, Sir Gawain, am ready, if he has any business with me."
"Wait there," roared a fierce voice.
Soon you shall have what I promised you once," and the Green Knight,
looking as he did when he came to Arthur's court,
came hurtling through a gap in the rocks.
In his hand he carried a huge new axe.

"I am glad that you keep your word, Sir Gawain,"
said the Green Knight,
"and have come to receive a blow without fighting back,
just as I did, a year ago."
"Do what you must," Gawain replied. "I will stand still,"
and he bent his head, showing no sign of fear.
Fiercely the Green Knight raised the axe,
and it came rushing down.
But Gawain could not help flinching a little,
and the Green Knight swerved the blade aside.
"Well, you cannot be Sir Gawain," he said scornfully,
"for they say that he is the bravest knight on earth.
Did I flinch when you cut off my head?
I must be a braver knight than you are."
"I will not flinch this time," said Gawain,
"though if you cut off my head
I cannot put it back again as you did."
Grimly the Green Knight prepared to strike,
but at the last moment he aimed the blow away,
though Gawain stood ready, as firm as a rock.
Then Gawain was angry and told the Green Knight
to stop his threats and strike the blow.
For the third time the Green Knight raised the axe.
It came hurtling down, but slowed at the end
so that Gawain received only a small cut on his neck.
At once he leapt away, seized his sword and put on his helmet,
and cried, "You have had your one blow!
If you strike me again, I am ready for battle."

The Green Knight rested on his axe and said cheerfully,
"Do not be so angry, Sir Gawain.
I promised you one blow, and one blow you have had.
My name is Sir Bertilak. I am the lord of the castle,
and the first two blows I aimed at you
were for the first two nights of our bargain,
when you gave me the kisses that my dear wife gave you.
The third night you were not quite true to your word,
for you kept secret my own green girdle that my wife gave to you.
I sent my wife to test you, and I know now
that you are the truest knight on earth.
You failed a little over the girdle, but who can blame you?
That was because you love your life and did not want to die."
He said that the ugly old lady, Morgan le Fay,
was a wicked enchantress who had sent the Green Knight
to test the famous courage of King Arthur's court.
She had even hoped that Guinevere might die of fright.
Gawain stood in silence, filled with great shame.
"This girdle has proved me both cowardly and greedy,"
he said sadly, handing it to the Green Knight.
But the Green Knight laughed,
and said he had paid for his faults,
and gave him the girdle to keep as a gift.

Then the Green Knight asked Gawain
to honour his company again at the castle,
but Gawain thanked him once more and said that he would
set out on the long journey back to Camelot.
After many adventures he reached Arthur's court,
and the company there was overjoyed to see him return.
He told them the story of all that had happened,
and showed them the cut on his neck,
and the lovely green girdle which he wore as a baldric.
"If ever I am proud of my skill in battle," he said,
"this baldric will remind me of my shame
when I was proved to be a coward."
But the company all praised him, and everyone agreed
to wear a green baldric from that day forever
in honour of Sir Gawain and the great courage he had shown
in the Green Knight's Christmas challenge.